The Boy Who Swallowed Snakes

BY LAURENCE YEP

ILLUSTRATED BY JEAN AND MOU-SIEN TSENG

SCHOLASTIC INC.

New York

Library of Congress Cataloging-in-Publication Data

Yep, Laurence.
    The boy who swallowed snakes / by Laurence Yep : illustrated
by Jean and Mou-sien Tseng.
      p. cm.
    Summary: A brave and honest young boy with an unusual
appetite for snakes turns the tables on a greedy rich man.
  ISBN 0-590-46168-0
  [1. Folklore—China.] I. Tseng, Jean, ill. II. Tseng, Mou-sien,
ill. III. Title
PZ8.1.Y37Bo 1993
398.21—dc20   93-21822
[398.2]   CIP
             AC
12 11 10 9 8 7 6 5 4 3 2 1   4 5 6 7 8 9/9
Printed in the U.S.A.   36

First Scholastic printing, February 1994

Designed by Claire B. Counihan

The illustrations in this book
are watercolor paintings.

To my great-nephew,
Esteban.
—L. YEP

For our niece and nephews,
Lindsay, Andrew, and Kevin,
who are a great joy to us.
—J. & M. TSENG

A LONG TIME AGO in southern China, forests still covered the hills. In their great, green shadow a small village huddled, and in that village lived a boy named Little Chou and his widowed mother. They were so poor that they had no land to farm.

One day as he searched the forest for something to eat, Little Chou spotted a tree that grew dragon's eyes. "That's mother's favorite fruit," he said to himself and climbed the tree. As he sat among the branches, Little Chou saw a man stumbling along the path beneath him. In his arms, he held a small basket of bamboo.

"How odd," Little Chou said to himself. "Though that man wears expensive silk robes, he has no servants to carry his load."

The rich man dropped the basket and hurried away. Curious, Little Chou climbed down and peeked inside. He found a silver bowl filled with silver coins.

Though he was very poor, Little Chou was also very honest. He ran after the man. "Hey," Little Chou panted, "you left your silver."

Instead of thanking him, the rich man got angry. "I don't leave my money lying around." With a strange smile he quickly left the forest.

Little Chou excitedly dragged the basket home. "Mama! We're rich!" he cried.

But Mrs. Chou screamed, "There's a snake on your leg!"

When he looked down, Little Chou saw a slender serpent coiled around his leg, glowing like a rope of blue light. Terrified, he threw the snake away and stamped on it.

In the wink of an eye the snake curled around his leg again. Its body was as good as new.

Little Chou and his mother tried to drown the snake in a pot of water, but it returned to the boy's leg. And it was dry.

They tried to burn it in the stove, but it came back again. And it was cool.

Little Chou limped to the house of the wise old woman. However, as soon as she saw Little Chou, the old woman grabbed a broom. "Don't bring that evil into my house. It's a *ku* snake."

Little Chou scratched his head. "What kind of snake is that?"

"It's part of the magic of the people who lived here before us," the old woman explained. "The snake kills people, steals their treasure and brings the wealth back to its owner. But the *ku* snake is so dangerous, the owner must have been too scared to keep it. He probably left silver to trick you into taking the snake. If you don't use the snake, the snake will become angry and kill you instead."

"I won't harm anyone," Little Chou said bravely. "I can't destroy the snake but I know one way to get rid of this evil." Little Chou swallowed the snake before anyone could stop him.

His mother slapped his back to make him spit it out. "Now you're going to die," she wailed.

"And it will be a horrible death," the wise woman predicted solemnly.

Little Chou stood still and waited to die while his mother wept. After a while, his feet began to ache so he sat down. And so did his mother. And so did the wise woman.

By sunset, his mother had cried out all her tears. Little Chou was beginning to feel embarrassed. "How much longer do I have to wait?" he asked the wise woman.

"By now you should have died gruesomely." The wise woman poked Little Chou with her broom. "I could have sworn that it was a *ku* snake."

Mrs. Chou sniffed. "Some people just can't handle being wrong."

"Some people just can't handle being cursed," the wise woman grumbled. "Quit cluttering up my doorway! Go away!"

When they returned home a light suddenly flashed out of Little Chou's stomach. It darted toward his mother. She ducked quickly. "What's that?" she asked.

The light zipped over her head, and streaked across the night sky like a meteor. Little Chou stared up in astonishment as the light split into two snakes, each about the size of Little Chou's forearm.

Little Chou seized a snake in each hand. "I'll get rid of them, just like the first," he said. He ate both snakes before his mother could stop him.

"That's enough. Come into the house now," said Mrs. Chou. "You're more likely to die of a cold than from a *ku* snake."

The next evening, Little Chou's stomach sparkled and then a light flashed out into the night sky. It burst like a rocket into fifty smaller flames. The lights turned into fifty snakes.

The snakes darted into the house. They played games upon the table and benches. They painted with soot from the brick stove. They drummed their tails against the pots. Their bodies glowed, filling the house with flickering lights.

Little Chou's mother blinked her eyes. "They're better than candles or oil lamps. I wish we could sell them."

"We'd sell the evil, too." Little Chou swept five snakes into his fist but his mother scolded him.

"Evil or not, you might as well eat them like a civilized person," she said. She gave him a rice bowl and a pair of chopsticks.

The next evening, there were a hundred snakes, each the size of Little Chou's index finger. They flew round and round like a flock of stars. "They're my little night lights," Little Chou said.

When he had collected all of them, he cheerfully fried them with a little garlic. "I've never had so much meat in my life."

He offered a helping to his mother but she declined. "I don't care for snake meat."

The following night, there were a thousand snakes, each the size of Little Chou's thumb. They flashed about the dark sky as if they were playing tag with the stars. These, Little Chou boiled in a spicy stew.

For ten nights, the snakes flashed through the air like tiny comets. It looked as if the stars had fallen from the sky and emptied into the courtyard.

"We must bury the snakes so deep they won't bother us," Mrs. Chou decided. "Who will help us?" she called out to the crowd.

A farmer named Ox slowly stepped forward. "For one piece of silver, I'll dig a hole deep as the well, but no amount of silver would make me touch those snakes."

After Farmer Ox dug the hole, he left with his piece of silver.

The very next day Farmer Ox went to town, but to his dismay, no one could make change for so much money.

"Go to Mr. Owyang. He's very rich," suggested a letter writer.

So Farmer Ox went to Mr. Owyang's mansion.

"Where did you get this silver piece?" demanded Mr. Owyang, who had recognized his own money.

"I earned it with my great courage," boasted Farmer Ox. "I helped a boy get rid of a house full of snakes."

Mr. Owyang grew thoughtful. "I got rid of the *ku* snake because I was afraid it would turn on me. But a mere boy has found a way to multiply the snakes. If one snake could make me wealthy, how much could ten thousand snakes steal? I must find this boy."

Mr. Owyang changed Farmer Ox's silver piece and sent him away. Then he called for his chair. "Follow that farmer back to his village," he ordered.

Little Chou's house was easy to find because thousands of tiny night lights dashed inside and outside, above and below. The snakes had zipped out of the ground at the same hour as they used to from Little Chou's stomach.

Mr. Owyang pushed his way through the crowd.

"What are you doing with my pets?" he demanded.

Little Chou picked up a basket. "So you admit that the snakes are yours?"

Mrs. Chou glared at Mr. Owyang. "And I suppose the silver is yours, too."

Mr. Owyang shook his head. "Keep the money. I'll have plenty more, soon enough."

The moment Little Chou handed his basket to Mr. Owyang, the night lights disappeared. Only one slender snake remained, coiled around the rich man's arm.

Mr. Owyang waved his arm. "Get it off me!" he shrieked.

Little Chou was puzzled. "You wanted it back. Besides, the snake never hurt me."

"Yes, of course," Mr. Owyang hastily replied. "But I expected more than one snake."

"You'll get more if you eat this one," Little Chou explained.

"Uh!" Mr. Owyang stared at the snake in disgust. The snake gazed back distastefully at him. "It didn't...disagree with your stomach?"

"Not at all. Try it with a little garlic and soy sauce," Little Chou suggested helpfully.

"I'm no country bumpkin," Mr. Owyang snapped back. "I'll eat it in a sauce fit for the emperor. Take me back to my mansion," he ordered his servants.

As soon as he returned home, Mr. Owyang announced a big celebration. "Tonight I'm going to become richer than the emperor," he bragged.

That night musicians and jugglers, acrobats, singers and dancers entertained Mr. Owyang while he sipped the finest wines from his favorite jade cup and nibbled rare delicacies from gold platters.

Because he trusted no one with his snake, Mr. Owyang commanded his chef to cook the snake at the banquet table.

However, the rich man's heart was greedy where Little Chou's heart had been pure. The instant Mr. Owyang took a bite, he felt a great pain in his stomach. He fell upon the table wriggling about on his belly. Dishes of food and jugs of wine were knocked to the floor. The servants ran screaming from the mansion, leaving their master to die alone on top of his banquet table.

And so the *ku* snake had its revenge on the greedy master who tried to abandon it.

As for Little Chou, he and his mother used the remaining silver to buy the most fertile land in the village. They planted rice fields with the finest seed they could find. And so they became wealthy through their wits and hard labor.

And though Little Chou was content with his good fortune, on clear nights, he would gather with his family and watch the servants set off fireworks until the sky seemed like a garden full of flashing stars.

But it was never the same as when he had his very own magical night lights.